D0246552

HAMMERSMITH AND FULHAM
3 8005 01621 807 0

WAVE

First published in 2016 in Great Britain by
Barrington Stoke Ltd
18 Walker Street, Edinburgh, EH3 7LP

www.barringtonstoke.co.uk

A CIP catalogue record for this book is available from the British Library upon request

ISBN: 978-1-78112-562-5

Printed in China by Leo

WAVE

PAUL DOWSWELL

Barrington Stoke

To my Hastings Pals,
Tony and Jan

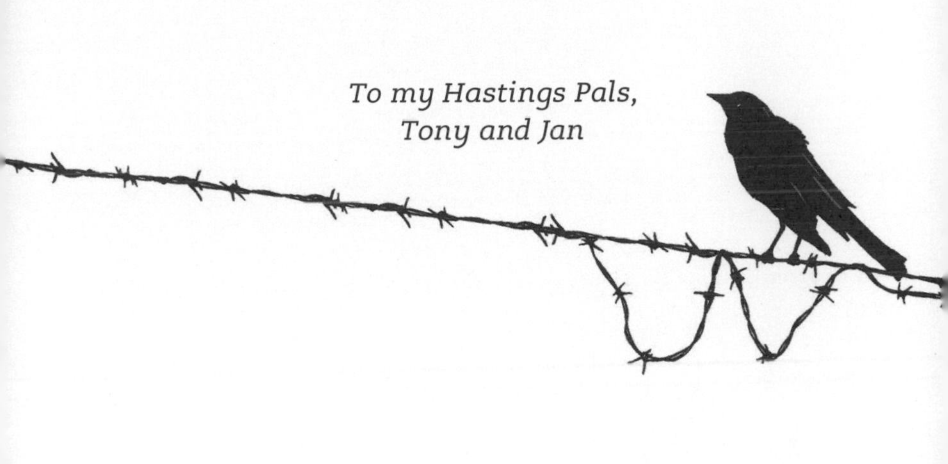

CONTENTS

Chapter 1 1

Chapter 2 7

Chapter 3 17

Chapter 4 25

Chapter 5 30

Chapter 6 35

Chapter 7 44

Chapter 8 47

Chapter 9 50

Chapter 10 61

Chapter 11 65

Chapter 12 72

Chapter 13 79

About the Pals in *Wave* 85

CHARACTERS

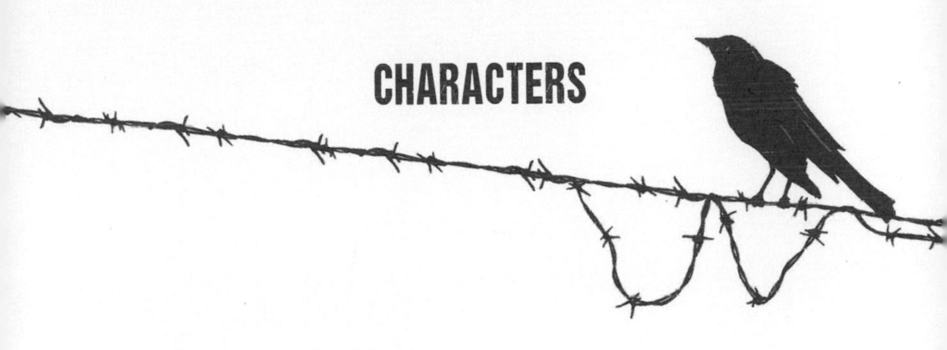

Hastings – July 2016

<u>Charlie and Eddie Taylor</u> – two brothers

<u>Rose Taylor</u> – Grandma Rose.
Grandmother to Charlie and Eddie

Hastings/The Somme – 1916

<u>Charlie and Eddie Taylor</u> – two brothers

<u>Rose</u> – Charlie's girlfriend, and destined to be mother to Grandma Rose

CHAPTER 1

Friday 1st July, 2016

The view out to sea is unsettling. Blazing sunshine smothers the beach in a lazy haze, but dark clouds hang heavy on the horizon to the east. Lightning flashes amid those clouds and a low rumble of thunder rolls over the waves towards the few people on the beach. It's the first of July and too early in the season for crowds of tourists. Charlie and his brother Eddie sit on the shingle and share a bottle of Fanta and a big meaty pasty.

"I reckon it's going away from us, Eddie," Charlie says. He wipes his fingers on his jeans.

“The French can have it,” Eddie says with a laugh. “We don’t want a thunderstorm spoiling our summer day.”

Charlie’s mobile pipes up with some cheesy pop song. He answers after a few bars. “Yeah, Poppy,” he says. “How’s it going?”

Eddie doesn’t want to intrude on his brother’s conversation and so he stares out to sea. He doesn’t like Poppy much, probably because he senses she doesn’t really like him. But she’s bright and pretty and Charlie is lucky to have her as a girlfriend. Eddie feels a stab of envy. He’d like a girl, especially one as fit as her.

He feels a stab of irritation too. He can hear Poppy’s voice, loud and stroppy over the phone.

“That daft brother of yours isn’t still thinking of joining the army, is he?” she says. “Tell him to stick it out in the real world. Don’t want him getting blown to bits.”

Eddie notices Charlie giving him an awkward sideways glance – hopeful perhaps that maybe he didn't hear that.

Eddie smiles to himself and thinks, 'OK, maybe she doesn't hate me after all.'

The conversation ends and a heavy silence hangs between the two brothers. Charlie breaks it. "Nice to be here though, ain't it," he says.

They've come down from London to help Grandma Rose clear out her elder sister's house. Great Aunt Lily lived to be 91 and died a good five years ago. The Taylor family have used the house as a holiday home ever since and no one could bear the thought of clearing it out and selling it.

Charlie has his eye on that old piano in the living room. The oak's a bit chipped, but they haven't got one at home and he likes to play when he gets the chance. But Eddie doesn't like that piano. He says it gives him the creeps. "Weirdo," Charlie calls him when he says that.

"Here look at this," Eddie says. He opens his sports bag and gets out a mottled photo held between two cardboard squares. "Found it in the attic. I wonder if it's worth anything?"

Charlie doesn't even look. "Stick it on eBay," he says.

"No, Charlie," Eddie says, "have a proper look. It's really interesting." Eddie is irritated by his brother's habit of not really listening to him. Charlie is only a year older – 18 to Eddie's 17 – but he treats Eddie like a child.

"You and your soldiers," Charlie says with a sigh. Eddie has been talking about joining the army for the last six months. It's always "army this army that" with him. He hasn't got a job, or a girlfriend, and their dad thinks the army will be the making of him.

But Charlie does look at the picture. Like the view out to sea, it's unsettling. British soldiers in a trench sit with their backs to a pile of sandbags. They all carry rifles with blades fixed to the barrels. Bright sunshine glints on the bayonets and on their steel helmets. The soldiers all have wide, frightened eyes that stare out at the camera from pale, thin faces.

"First World War, I reckon," Eddie says.

"Jesus, they look worried," says Charlie. "Think they're about to go into action?"

"Why else would they look like that?" says Eddie. He sighs. "I'd guess most of them are about the same age as us."

"Look at him, Eddie. He's a cool one."

Charlie has spotted the odd one out. One of the soldiers stares at the camera with anger rather than fear written across his face. He's slouched down on the muddy floor of the trench, next to a younger boy. The younger boy's face is the same as his, only softer and more troubled.

"Reckon they might be related," Eddie says.

“Might even be related to us,” says Charlie. “The one staring at the camera looks like Grandma Rose’s dad. Our mum reckons I look like him, and you do too a bit. Let’s take it back and ask her.”

“Later,” says Eddie. “Let’s sit out here a while longer. Those thunder clouds aren’t coming our way, at least not yet.”

His brother nods and his head dips forward in the blazing hot sun. Lulled by the steady rhythm of the waves, Charlie and Eddie are both asleep within minutes.

CHAPTER 2

Saturday 1st July, 1916
7.00 a.m.
The Western Front

It was a beautiful morning. The best they'd had all week. Today the dawn brought only dew, rather than mist and drizzle. There was still a chill in the air, but you could tell the day was going to be a scorcher. Charlie checked his water bottle to make sure it was full. Six months in the trenches had taught him that hot days like these meant a raging thirst if you weren't properly prepared.

He looked at the watch on his wrist. Half an hour to go. What might he be doing on a day like this, if he was back at home in Hastings? Maybe he'd still be in bed, while the sunlight nudged him awake through the gaps in the curtains. And if he was up, he'd be out there with Eddie, heading off to fish in the lake at Newgate Wood. Or he might be planning on taking a picnic to Bexhill with his girl Rose, picking their way along the path by the coast. When they did that they had to tell her parents they were going into London to look at the museums and do some shopping. Rose's parents wouldn't allow her to go off to the countryside with a boy. You never knew what they might get up to. Charlie smiled at the memory of it. Then he felt sad. This wasn't the sort of day to go to war.

The sky above might be cloudless blue but it was full of artillery shells. Charlie stared up and strained to spot them, even though he knew they moved too fast to see. This artillery bombardment had been going for six days now.

Non-stop shells screaming overhead and exploding on the German front line less than half a mile away. The men had been told it was to scare the buggers over there and keep them awake all night so they'd be a pushover when the Sussex boys arrived to take them on. Charlie allowed himself a grim little chuckle. Typical hare-brained thinking from the top brass. Even a child in their first year at Infant School would realise the non-stop shelling would keep British soldiers awake too. He felt so tired he could lie down and sleep in a pool of muddy water. He'd almost welcome death if it meant he could rest those battle-weary bones of his.

His thoughts turned to the coming attack. It was set for half past seven. Less than half an hour before that whistle blew, the whistle that would send them over the top. Were these really going to be the last minutes of his life? He thought of home, the smell of his mum's Sunday dinners, of lying on Hastings beach with Rose's head on his chest, and he felt a sad ache for the simple life he'd had before all this. He'd thought he was bored then – that was one reason he had volunteered. He'd give anything to be bored now.

He looked over to his younger brother, Eddie. Life in the trenches was hitting Eddie far harder than Charlie. Every time a shell exploded near by, Eddie's eyes twitched and he shuddered with horror. Charlie wondered how he was going to cope when they went over the top. Charlie would have enough on his own plate trying to keep himself alive, never mind looking after Eddie too. But a promise was a promise, and Charlie had promised his mum that Eddie would come back from France alive.

Charlie ran his hands over his jacket pockets looking for a letter from his girl Rose, and he found something else he'd forgotten he had. A nice thick slice of fruit cake. Yesterday, one of the lads had had a cake delivered from home. That was one of the funny things about the trenches. Your wife or your sweetheart – or your mum if you were still just a kid like Eddie – could be at home in their kitchen baking you a cake, then they'd pop it in a tin and take it down the Post Office. Three or four days later, it was there with you on the front line – still fresh enough to smell that lovely sweet 'just baked' smell. A gift from somewhere clean and safe over the Channel – a world away from the mud and stench of the trenches. It was hard to imagine that world now. Somewhere where people were kind and civil. Somewhere where a knife was something you used to slice a loaf, not to skewer someone's guts. Somewhere where you had an outside lavatory in your garden, rather than a stinking pit of a latrine in the support trench behind you, which you had to share with hundreds of men who had forgotten their manners long ago. Charlie tried not to think about the time he'd gone there to find Private Morgan sitting stone dead with his trousers round his ankles, the top of his head sheared off by a shrapnel shard.

Charlie held the slice of cake in his hands and thought about the kitchen where it had been baked. It seemed as unreachable as the Moon.

There had been a letter with the cake too, saying they could all hear the British artillery pounding the Huns. They said you could even hear it in London. A terrible, endless roar, louder than thunder. 'No flaming wonder they can hear it,' Charlie thought, listening to it now.

"What the hell was that?" One of the lads jumped to his feet. He looked even paler than the rest. "Something landed in the trench," he said and pointed. "Just missed me foot!"

Another lad got up and picked it out of the dry soil. He screeched in pain. "Jesus, it's hot," he said. He shook his hand in agony, and looked at the heavy steel object with horror. "That's a fuse from one of our shells," he said. "They shouldn't fall out like that. Shell won't explode without a fuse."

Charlie turned away and wondered how many of those shells had been as badly made as that one. He'd tease his Rose about that, if he ever saw her again. She worked in a factory that made shells.

He took a swig of his precious water to slake his thirst and bit into his slice of fruit cake. The wonderful rich taste of it made him think about the day he had left England. The Hastings Pals had formed up in neat rows in Wellington Square, just like the other battalions from all over the country that had sailed to France on the ferry. Rose had come to wave him off, but he had ignored her. They'd had a terrible row the day before. She'd never told him before that she didn't want him to go. She had always said how proud she was that he'd lied about his age to volunteer. But now he was leaving, it all came out. Why hadn't he stayed at school to do his exams? He could have sat the war out. You were supposed to be 18 to join the army. He was two years underage. And what was he doing taking

Eddie along, too, as if it was some kind of picnic? Eddie was a year younger – three years younger than he should have been to join up.

"It's sheer bloody murder," Rose had yelled at him in a fury, "taking a boy like your Eddie along."

Charlie had never heard her swear before. He didn't think girls like Rose said words like that. He'd raised his voice back at her, said things that shouldn't have been said and couldn't be undone. And so she had come to see him off and he wouldn't look at her properly, not even when he heard her call out. She'd sounded upset, desperate even.

But on the ferry over, Charlie had sat by himself on the top deck and watched the English coast grow further away. He regretted the way he'd acted now. And he started to question himself. After all, this might well turn out to be a one-way trip. Why had he joined up? *Why?* To fight for King and Country, he supposed. To defend our way of life against the savage Huns, to protect his Rosie, like the recruitment poster had said. But did he really think that or was he just after glory and more money in his pay packet?

The army certainly paid a lot more than Charlie earned as an apprentice carpenter. Maybe he was scared people would think he was a coward if he didn't go. Or a conshie – one of those men that said they wouldn't fight because they didn't believe in war. That's what he'd called Eddie, when he'd strong-armed him into joining up. Eddie didn't want anyone to think he was a coward, especially not Charlie.

Charlie had sorted it out with Rose, of course. He had written to her from France, as soon as they were allowed to. He was sorry he'd been such an ass, he said. She didn't forgive him so fast – she made him wait for a reply. But a month later she sent him a cake just like the one he was eating now, with a letter telling him how much she missed him. Knitted socks, scarves, another cake or two, had arrived over the months in training. But he'd not heard from her now since the start of June, and he was wondering if there was another boy back at home who'd caught her eye. Some handsome, sensible lad who hadn't rushed to join up.

CHAPTER 3

7.10 a.m.

"It's going to be a pushover, isn't it, Charlie?" Eddie said. His eyes searched his brother's face for reassurance.

They'd already had this conversation several times, and Charlie tried to keep his irritation in check as he waited for it to start again. Eddie had this habit of parroting the phrases the officers used when they briefed the men. Charlie called it "eyewash" – but Eddie didn't have that bullshit detector. He was too trusting, and so he wanted to believe everything he was told. It was like he felt it was his patriotic duty, that questioning things was the sort of "conshie" talk traitors used. Charlie used to think that too, back home – when he heard stories about conshies being given a good kicking when the pubs shut. He'd had no time for the men who refused to fight. Do-gooders, prats or anarchists, most of them, the newspapers said. Now that Charlie was sitting in the trench, waiting for the whistle, it was too late to admit that the conshies may have had a point.

The day before, the last day in June, they had all been ordered to form a huge three-sided square four miles behind the front line. Then some high-ranking nob on a horse had trotted into the middle of them to deliver a speech. He was the regimental Colonel, they were told. His riding boots gleamed in the sun.

The speech, to Charlie's ears, was pure bullshit. It did nothing to make him feel better about the battle they all knew was coming. But Eddie had lapped it all up. The Colonel had told them that barbed wire was the infantry's worst enemy and this artillery barrage, the one that had been going on for ever, would work like "a large broom" to get rid of it. It was sweeping the battle field clean of both the wire and the Huns, for the infantry to advance – that was them.

"First the artillery devastates and then the infantry overwhelms," the Colonel said. "That is our cardinal principal."

Many of the soldiers nodded wisely. Charlie thought most of them hadn't got the first idea what a "cardinal principal" was. He certainly hadn't. Maybe if he'd stayed on at school he would know.

Then the Colonel said he had some good news for them. They were going to have the honour of being part of the "First Wave". At 7.30 the next morning they would be among the first men to go into action in the "Big Push" – the battle that would win the war. The First Wave would have it easy, according to the Colonel.

"You will be at the German front line in five or ten minutes," he told them, "where you will dig in and wait for reinforcements. There will be thousands of your brothers in arms, right behind you."

The Germans would all be dead, or too stunned to defend themselves, the Colonel said. It would be "a walk in the park". As he listened, Charlie wondered if the Colonel had ever even seen the No Man's Land between the trenches. It was pocked with shell-crater pools of stinking mud and mangled, rotting bodies. The only place a "park" like that could exist was in the hell of his worst nightmares.

The Colonel went on to say they might find a few little patches of resistance. "Your job, my good men, will be to mop up those resistors."

It made it all sound like cleaning the kitchen floor, a task that belonged back in the safe world of baking cakes or cooking the dinner on a sunny afternoon.

Charlie hoped the Colonel was right, but his gut instinct told him that this walk in the park would be more like walking the plank. He burned with a sudden resentment towards the Colonel. He wanted to ask whether *he* was coming with them across No Man's Land, or whether he was going to wait the whole thing out at his HQ in a French castle, a safe distance away from the front line.

Then, when they were on the march back to their support trench close to the Front, Charlie had spotted a huge pit, freshly dug by the side of the road. The soil around two of its edges was at least as high as a man. As they approached, the sergeant shouted, "Eyes left", but he was too late. Most of them would have seen it – a great burial pit awaiting the dead. The sight of that pit destroyed any last spark of hope Charlie had about today's battle.

Now, Eddie was parroting the Colonel's words, as if they would keep him safe.

"Mopping up ..."

"A large broom ..."

“And those training exercises went really well,” Eddie said. “We all know exactly what to do.”

Eddie was right. They had been training these last few weeks – out in fields way behind the lines. Men with big red flags had walked ahead of them to indicate where the artillery shells of the “creeping barrage” would fall. Then there were lines of tape to show where the enemy trenches would be.

‘That creeping barrage sounds like a good idea at least,’ Charlie thought. It was a shield of artillery shells, falling maybe 50 yards ahead of them, moving forward towards the enemy at walking speed. That might even work. But the line of tape for the enemy trench was a joke. This would be a trench protected by rows and rows of lethal barbed wire and defended by Germans with machine guns. Charlie looked at his bayonet glinting in the sun and realised that the German soldiers had a very similar sort of blade on the end of their rifles. What would it feel like to have one of those thrust into your guts?

Charlie knew about the German trenches from first-hand experience. He'd never taken part in a full-scale assault like this one, but he had been on night raiding parties before. None of the Hastings boys had ever been in a full-scale assault.

Eddie was still jabbering on. "It's going to be a walkover," he said. "Literally."

Charlie didn't trust himself to speak, so he smiled at his younger brother and tried to hide his irritation.

That was the other piece of bullshit that the Colonel had spouted. The Hastings Pals were to line up out there in No Man's Land, and *walk* over. Out there, where just putting your head above the top of the trench would get you a bullet in the brain. But, of course, this morning the Huns would be too stunned or too dead to take aim at British soldiers.

"There will be no German soldiers firing on you," the Colonel had said.

Charlie had been told that so many times, he almost believed it.

CHAPTER 4

7.20 a.m.

A *walk* over.

Charlie thought of the gear they'd ordered him to take with him when he went over. He'd be walking not running with that. He'd be carrying equipment that weighed at least 60 pounds. That was like carting round his 9-year-old cousin, Thomas. As well as his usual rifle and ammo, backpack and all the rest, he'd be carrying the bottom half of a trench mortar, and some heavy-duty wire cutters. Wire cutters? The bombardment was supposed to have destroyed the barbed wire in front of the enemy trenches.

Why did he need them then? It was just one more thing about this grand plan that didn't add up.

Charlie's thoughts were interrupted by a commotion further down the line. The sergeants were handing out the morning rum ration and men were crowding round, jostling and eager for a shot of spirits before the battle. Each man had his own little cup, and the sergeants poured the rum carefully from a hefty clay jug. Eddie's face lit up – he liked the way the rum made him feel. After his morning shot he was always cheerful for a while. But Charlie was wary of it. The only way to survive in such a dangerous place was to keep your wits about you. Drink was for evenings in the pub – not mornings in a battle trench.

Today they were giving the men double rations – not enough to get them drunk, but more than enough to chase away the fear that gnawed like rats at their guts. Eddie knocked back his two tots as fast as he could. Charlie took one and refused the second.

"That's more like it," Eddie said, and his eyes shone. He paced up and down restlessly and hugged a few of his pals, wishing them luck in the ordeal ahead.

Five minutes later Eddie fell silent, and Charlie could tell he was fighting back tears. "How are we going to get out of this scrap?" he whispered. "We've had it, Charlie, haven't we?"

Charlie put an arm around him. He could sense his brother was trying to hold in great bursting sobs. He cursed the rum and wished, too, that he'd been more hopeful about their chances. Maybe then Eddie wouldn't be so scared.

Charlie thought hard. Could they hide somewhere out in No Man's Land? There were plenty of craters out there. The ground was almost like honeycomb. But the officers would be watching them. Anyone who didn't "do his duty" faced being shot. And so did anyone who stayed behind when the whistle blew. They all knew about that. A minute or two after that whistle,

Military Police marched down into the trenches and shot anyone who was still there. You had to be a right bastard to do that job, Charlie had always thought.

"Come on, Eddie," he said. "Chin up. Don't let your mates see you like this."

All at once the thunder stopped. Peace descended. It was like a miracle.

But this was it. The attack was about to begin. Men started to fix ladders to the side of the trenches. Sergeants were shouting orders, barking like hearty sheepdogs herding their flock.

Harry Pike – a skinny lad with snaggle teeth who they'd been to school with – looked over at Charlie and Eddie. "Smile, yer miserable buggers," he called.

"Leave us alone, Harry," Charlie snapped.

But Harry ignored him and took a shot on his Brownie camera.

Charlie could hear birds tweeting, and even wind rustling in the leaves of the few bushes and saplings that survived in the field beyond the trench. Now they were only moments away from going over the top in the First Wave. Charlie felt like he was standing on the edge of a huge cliff, peering down into a dizzy void.

CHAPTER 5

Hastings
Saturday 1st July, 1916
7.30 a.m.

Rose woke with a start. She had only drifted off half an hour ago, after she got home from her night shift at the shell factory. Saturday was her only day off, and all she wanted to do was catch up on her sleep. But something was wrong. She sensed it deep in her bones. Then she realised what it was. The endless rolling thunder of artillery that had been drifting over from France all the last week had stopped. She looked at her watch. 7.30 exactly. Her gut clenched with an anxiety that was almost too much to bear.

'Charlie,' she thought, her heart pounding. 'My Charlie! Is he about to go into action? And that irritating little brother of his too?'

Then she felt a sudden pang of guilt. Why hadn't she written to him more? It had been weeks now since her last letter. She had been working so hard in the factory, making shells for the artillery. When she got home after working all night, she was too tired to write Charlie a letter, never mind bake him a cake. There was a big push on making those shells. It was all top secret, but the girls she worked with wondered if a great battle was being planned out on the Western Front. Then, a week ago, they heard that thunder from the east, rolling over the Channel, and they knew they had been right.

"When that stops, that's when the real battle will begin," her friend Vera had said.

What Vera didn't say, but they all thought it, was that was also when the telegrams would start to arrive. The ones with black borders that told you your loved ones had been killed.

Rose liked Vera and the girls she worked with, but it was a funny job in that factory. You felt you were 'doing your bit' as the poster said when she applied. Other than that, Rose didn't always feel she knew quite what she was doing. But the wages were far more than she could hope to earn working in a shop. Five quid a week! It was a fortune. For the first time in her life, Rose had money to spend on herself. Sometimes the girls would go out in an evening, on their own, without men, and have a drink in a pub.

They even talked about setting up their own football team. "We could call ourselves the Hastings Harridans," Vera had said with a grin. Rose loved the idea of playing football. No one would have said a word about it if there were husbands and boyfriends and brothers around to scoff. It wasn't all bad, having the men away.

Rose saved her wages, too. She wanted to buy a nice little house with Charlie when he got back. He hadn't said anything about marrying her, yet. But in her mind he was the one for her. So she was going to keep that nest egg a secret until he did.

But Rose knew that the factory job paid well because it was a mixed blessing. It was dangerous. All those chemicals. All those explosives. A single accident could blow the whole building sky high and shatter every window in town.

"It's like being in a box of fireworks," her friend Ada had said. And she was right, so they never talked about it. But then something would happen at a factory somewhere else, and they'd read about it in the papers. A building razed to the ground. A hundred killed in a flash, and maybe five or six hundred injured. Rose always had nightmares after she read those stories.

And the work turned your skin yellow, especially if you worked with that chemical they called TNT. In the shops and the streets, they called the factory workers "canary girls" because of it, like it was a big joke. Rose didn't think it was funny at all. She was sure that anything that changed your skin colour was bad for you, apart from the sun. But the factory bosses told them it wouldn't harm them at all.

"Ladies," they said, "stop your fussing. There's a war on, so let's get those shells made with the greatest haste."

But Rose felt they had been making those shells so fast that she was sure they couldn't have been doing a proper job of it at all.

CHAPTER 6

Saturday 1st July, 1916
7.30 a.m.

In the stillness that followed the end of the artillery barrage, time seemed to slow down.

Charlie sensed every breath, every beat of his thumping heart. He turned his face up and the sun felt warm and gentle on his skin. As he looked at the blue sky through the narrow confines of the trench, a bird flew over. The sunlight flickered on its pale lower wings and that ordinary, everyday sight seemed like the most beautiful thing he had ever seen.

Then, with the next beat of the bird's wings, the world fell into darkness and panic. A massive explosion shook the ground and rent the air. A vast pillar of earth rose into the sky and blotted out the sun, still shallow on the horizon. A rain of pebbles, clods of earth, roots, and a hundred other things, fell into the British front line.

Some of the soldiers laughed out loud. "That should give Fritz an almighty shock," said Harry Pike.

"What the hell was it?" said Charlie.

"Mines under the German lines," Harry said with a knowing look. "We've been digging them for months. Packed full of explosives. Top secret surprise, innit! We've blown the buggers to kingdom come."

"Prepare to scale," a sergeant shouted. And, in the midst of chaos, the soldiers formed an orderly line by the ladders.

As they stood there, the stillness and the silence returned. Charlie thought of the last time he saw Rose, down at the harbour in Hastings and how he had ignored her. That slight now seemed as brutal and heartless as the bird overhead had been beautiful. He would give anything to hold her in his arms, give her one last kiss.

The officers were staring at their watches. Then the first whistle blew. They could hear the harsh peep of them all down the line.

"Form up," the sergeants shouted. And the soldiers obeyed them.

'It's like a drill in the parade ground,' Charlie thought in despair. 'As if it will do us any good marching over in a straight line, all steady like.'

And so Charlie hung back as the neat lines of soldiers climbed their wooden ladders. He was in no hurry to be among the first to go "over the top". But the strange silence hung in the air. The brave souls who were now out in the open weren't being shot at.

Charlie reached for the base plate and the leg tube of the Stokes Trench Mortar he was to carry over No Man's Land. The leg tube would steady the mortar barrel as it fired. His friend, John Roberts, was carrying the barrel of the mortar. John was a pal from a few streets away in Hastings who had been born on the same day as him. It was a fair distribution of weight.

There was still no gunfire from the Germans, even though there must be hundreds of men now, all along the line in front of their trenches, out there in plain sight. The walking didn't seem such a bad idea, after all.

Charlie took the weight of the base plate and asked Eddie to pass the leg tube up to him when he got to the top of the ladder. But Eddie was cowering in the bottom of the trench, all curled up, arms around his hunched legs. Tears streamed down his face and he was biting his hand in terror.

Charlie spoke to him, his voice soft but urgent. “Come on, Eddie. Look lively. We’ve got to get up this ladder.”

His words did not register.

Charlie spoke a little louder. “Come on, Eddie. Look, the Fritzes are all dead. No one’s shooting at us!”

His words were blotted out by a burst of machine-gun fire over to the east. A dark stain spread around Eddie’s crotch. He’d wet himself.

‘Oh, for God’s sake,’ Charlie thought, in a rage of embarrassment and fear for his brother. The base plate was heavy in his arms and he was losing patience. “Eddie, come on,” he begged. “It’s nothing – was probably one of ours. You’ve got to move, or they’ll shoot you on the spot.”

Charlie hefted the base plate up beyond the parapet and caught sight of John Roberts, already out there in front of the trench. “Stick close to me, Charlie,” John shouted.

Charlie's temper snapped. "Give me the rest of it," he shouted down to Eddie. "Now!"

At last, Eddie got to his feet and passed Charlie the leg tube. Charlie grabbed it, then watched in despair as his brother collapsed onto his backside again.

Charlie looked to his left down the trench. A distance away he caught sight of men with yellow bands on their peaked caps. The Military Police. He heard angry yelling, and then the sharp retort of a pistol.

"Eddie, stay there and you're dead," he shouted. "Come with me and you might live."

Another shot rang out, closer now.

Eddie screwed up his face in blind determination and scrambled to his feet. Charlie reached out a hand and dragged his brother up the ladder.

Out there in No Man's Land the morning sun was casting long black shadows on the cratered earth. The First Wave had already set off on their walk across the half-mile that separated them from the German trenches.

"Charlie, I forgot my sandbag," Eddie said. "I've got to go back for it. Sergeant Baker will have me on a charge."

Charlie knew he was right – everyone had been ordered to carry something. The hefty sandbags were for extra protection when they reached the enemy trenches.

But what he said was, "Bollocks to that. Here, you carry the leg tube."

They stumbled across the shattered landscape. Neither of them had ever seen it in daylight. They'd only been out in darkness – on wire repair duty – and Eddie had never volunteered for the night-time raiding parties. Charlie sometimes wondered why he had. Excitement, he supposed, and the chance to win a medal to impress his Rose.

All along the Front, as far as their eyes could see, there were steady lines of infantry men walking forward. Charlie felt his heart soar. It was odd, but it was a magnificent sight. The "creeping barrage" they had been told to expect hadn't happened, although further down the line to the south, Charlie could see shells exploding in No Man's Land. 'Maybe this is for the best,' he thought. The idea that they'd follow just behind a curtain of shells had always sounded as risky as hell.

A few shells exploded in the distance, behind the German lines, which were marked by dense thickets of barbed wire. The artillery broom hadn't swept the land as clean as that Colonel on his high horse had claimed. Charlie felt grateful he had his wire cutters strapped to his chest.

Just then, Eddie let out a yelp and Charlie wondered if he had been hit. Ahead of them, in the mangled earth, was a rotting corpse. It had a horrible grin on its decaying face, and its skeletal limbs were splayed this way and that, like a doll dropped on the floor by a careless child. In the sharp morning light they became aware of all the other festering corpses of No Man's Land. This truly was a kingdom of the dead.

"Watch your feet and keep looking ahead, Eddie," Charlie warned. "We're half way there already."

But the silence was unsettling him. The Germans still hadn't opened fire on them. Was the man on the horse right about that at least? Were they all really dead after all?

CHAPTER 7

Friday 1st July, 2016

"Boys, come on, wake yourselves. You'll not sleep at night if you doze off now!"

Eddie and Charlie shake their weary heads. It's Grandma Rose, come down to the beach to look for them.

"It's hard work, clearing out an attic," Eddie says with a smile.

"I know," says Grandma Rose, "but you're going home tonight and I need you back at the house before you go."

"In a minute," Charlie says.

"Here, Grandma, do you know who these people are?" Eddie asks and he shows her the old photo.

A look of sadness crosses her face and she pauses a moment before asking, "Where did you find this? I've never seen it before."

Before they can answer, Grandma Rose tells them the soldier is her father. He's the one with the intense, angry stare. "You're named after him, Charlie," Grandma Rose says. "And the one next to him is his younger brother Eddie." She looks at Eddie and nods.

"So, that makes Charlie our great-grandfather? And Eddie our great-great-uncle?" Charlie says. "Poor old Eddie looks bloody scared."

Grandma Rose heaves a sad sigh. "He had every reason to be," she says. "He was only just sixteen."

They sit in silence for a while, listening to the waves churning on the shore. Neither Charlie or Eddie feels like asking what happened to him.

"He never talked about the war, my dad," Grandma Rose says. "Never talked much about anything, to be honest. He certainly never showed me this picture. I don't think my mum even saw it. Maybe it was taken at the Somme. I know him and Eddie were both there. Horrible great battle, that was. Tens of thousands of men sent like lambs to the slaughter. The Somme." Grandma Rose pauses, as if she is overwhelmed by the word itself. "I imagine that's where it was taken."

CHAPTER 8

Saturday 1st July, 1916
7.30 a.m.

Over in the German lines, men had cowered for an entire week under a bombardment that had driven some of them gibbering mad. Now, at 7.30 a.m. on the dot, that endless shelling had stopped. It was as if someone had simply flicked a switch. The stillness could only mean one thing.

Attack.

In the silence that followed there was a frantic dash to be ready.

But the officers were wary. What if this was a ruse to lure them out and then begin shelling again? It was too obvious, surely, to stop at 7.30 a.m. exactly.

As they looked at each other, uncertain, the huge rumble of a mine blast shook the ground, filling some of the dug-outs with a storm of choking dust and earth.

They weren't uncertain any more. This was it. The British were attacking. If they'd had time to think, the German soldiers who survived the mine explosion would have felt grateful it wasn't on their section of the line. The men caught by the explosion wouldn't have stood a chance.

Now, men swung from their bunks, pulled on greatcoats and helmets, and raced up the sturdy wooden stairs of their deep dug-outs to take their places in the deserted trenches. The devastation that greeted them wasn't as intense as the shock of the bombardment had led them to believe. They breathed in glorious lungfuls of fresh air, delighted to be away from the awful reek of their hide-outs underground. They could see their trenches had stood up pretty well to the shelling. As the machine-gun teams set up their deadly weapons on the trench parapets, they were also relieved to see the dense barbed wire that protected the ground in front of them was very much intact. It had moved around a little – it wasn't exactly where it had been laid – but it was still there, and it was still just as effective.

Now they could see British soldiers walking towards them, bright shapes stark in the morning sun.

"Why don't they run?" one astonished Kapitän said, as his men fumbled with their machine-gun tripods and fed their cartridge web belts into the guns. But they were frantic, too hasty to do the job well.

"*Schnell!* Quick!" the Kapitän shouted. "Or we shall all die at the point of a British bayonet. Be ready, but hold your fire until I give the order."

CHAPTER 9

Saturday 1st July, 1916
7.40 a.m.

“Colonel was right,” Harry Pike said, as Charlie and Eddie caught up with him. “It’s a walk in the park all right.”

The men were advancing now, with rifles held out in front of them. The rifles were long, lethal and tipped with bayonets that glinted in the sun.

But Charlie’s keen eyes spotted heads bobbing in the trenches in front of them. “Their barbed wire’s held,” he shouted. “We’re for it now.”

A young lieutenant turned and looked at him with pure anger. "Silence in the ranks," he snapped.

Charlie noticed that Eddie was lagging behind and he waved his arms, urging him to keep up. His brother looked lifeless already, with his white face and blank eyes staring into nothing. He moved forward like one of the undead.

The line faltered at the first thicket of dense barbed wire.

"What now?" Harry Pike muttered and the young lieutenant called over to Charlie, "Taylor, get to work."

Charlie dropped his mortar stand, fell to his stomach and began to cut away at the wire.

At that very moment a German machine gun opened up right in front of them. Its bullets swept along the line, and Charlie's companions fell like nine-pins knocked over by a steel whip. Eddie was standing right next to Charlie, and he fell face first onto the dense thicket of barbed wire Charlie was trying to cut. Charlie reached up to try to untangle him, but bullets spattered around him. Instinct made him roll into a shallow shell crater where the machine-gun fire could not reach him.

But over the bark of the guns, Charlie could hear Eddie's voice, cracking with fear and pain as he cried out desperately for help. "Charlie, Charlie, you've got to get me out of this."

In a flash Charlie remembered a time, maybe five or six years before, when they were playing at school in Hastings. They had decided to climb onto the roof for a dare. Eddie shimmied up a drain pipe, no problem, but then he lost his nerve two thirds of the way up. He'd called out just as desperately for help then too. Charlie had had to rescue him. How was he going to do that now?

"Eddie, keep still," he called, as loudly as he dared. "If you shout out they'll shoot you again. You've got to wait for the next lot of our boys to arrive."

There was no reply.

'Is he taking my advice – or has he died?' Charlie thought. He felt like he was in a dream. Like this wasn't really happening. Machine guns rattled as they spat out ten bullets a second. Charlie's mind was racing. What could he do? Even if the Germans didn't shoot Eddie on purpose, he would be caught in the cross fire when more British troops arrived. Charlie had to do something. He reached for a grenade in his belt, and lobbed it over to the German trench in front of him. As he waited for it to explode he heard something he never expected – mocking laughter. The blast followed a second later. But his ears told him it was outside – not inside – the trench. Someone had caught his grenade and thrown it back out again.

Charlie took a second grenade and counted to four before he threw it. It had a seven-second fuse. This time the muffled blast told him he had hit his target. Before the *boom* faded from his ears he rushed out to Eddie, and tried to untangle his body from the barbed wire.

Eddie couldn't speak but his eyes pleaded with his brother as machine-gun bullets thudded into the ground around them. Then he cried out in agony as a bullet cut through his body.

Charlie threw himself back into his crater. He had stirred up a hornets' nest. Grenades and mortar bombs rained down on him. One "potato masher" grenade landed at his shoulder. Without a second thought Charlie flipped it over the lip of the crater and it exploded a few feet away. He had only one hope. He had to make the German soldiers think he was dead. He lay still while Eddie begged him for help, and he lay still while his brother begged him to tell him he was still alive.

"Charlie, tell me you're not dead. Tell me you're still alive and I can die in peace," Eddie cried in distress.

Charlie couldn't bring himself to answer.

The machine guns opened up again, and their violent *ra-ta-tat-tat* punctured the air around him. The second wave were coming.

A British soldier fell into Charlie's crater, clutching his stomach. Charlie crawled over to help him, but the man died within seconds. Three, then four other soldiers crowded in, then a fifth who didn't make it as far as the shelter of the rim where Charlie lay. A burst of bullets around his body told the men that the far side of their scant hiding place was in the enemy gunners' line of fire. The blood of the fifth man seeped into the dry earth as he died.

One of the new arrivals was an officer. "We can't stay here, boys," he said. "We've got to press on."

"But, Sir, it's murder," another of the soldiers replied. "The wire is still there. The Germans are still there. We'll be killed the moment we stick our heads up out of this stinking crater."

The officer fixed him with a glare.

'He's just a boy really,' Charlie thought, 'but he won't stand for anyone going against his orders.' Charlie knew his type. Once a year, his school had played the local private school at cricket. The boys there were well mannered, and he almost liked them, except for this formidable superiority and confidence they had. This young officer had it too, in spades.

"When I count to three, you are all to follow me," he said.

Charlie admired his pluck, if not his tactics. He cut in. "Sir, shall we wait for the next wave, then join them? We'll be cut down in seconds if just the four of us show ourselves."

The officer listened and this time he decided this stranger was right. "Good sense, Private," he said. "Good sense. They'll be along in the next five minutes. That's the plan, I'm told."

Then the officer looked up. "What the devil is that noise?" he asked in horror.

"It's my brother, Sir. He's caught on the wire," said Charlie.

"Poor blessed soul," the officer said. "Have you tried to help him?"

"Several times," Charlie said and at once he felt a hot rush of shame at his lie.

The men fell silent. They reloaded their rifles and took long gulps from their water bottles. The sun was higher in the sky now, and it was swelteringly hot.

Despite the water, Charlie felt parched. 'More than anything,' he thought, 'I'd like to drink a whole jug of iced water then throw myself into the sea on Hastings beach.' The image of the cool salty sea ebbed away as he realised with horror how thirsty Eddie must be. What could he do to help him?

Time passed in an agony of waiting. Tension etched itself deep into the soldiers' faces as they listened to the groans of wounded men all around them.

Then there were shouts in the distance. It was the approach of the third wave.

The officer drew his revolver from its leather pouch. “On my command,” he said.

Charlie felt sick to his stomach. He knew what would happen. As soon as they came out of that crater he would be swept away. He prayed death would meet him in a quick burst of fire and he wouldn’t end up hanging on the wire like poor Eddie.

“*Now*,” the officer said, and he led the way out of the crater as the third wave was almost on top of them. Another soldier leaped out after him and both were cut down in an instant. The officer fell back into the crater, half in and half out. Another burst of machine-gun fire shook his body, but he was already dead.

Charlie looked at the other two soldiers crouching next to him. "Good thing we weren't so keen," the older soldier said. Charlie recognised that accent. He was Scottish.

"*Shush!*" Charlie told him. "Quiet! Remember we're within grenade range of the German trench."

"I'm all for staying here until it's dark," the Scotsman whispered. "Then we can crawl back to our trenches."

Charlie and the other soldier nodded their heads. What else could they do but sit it out in this strange hell?

Then there was a lull, and Charlie concluded that somebody in charge was wondering whether to send another wave of men out to face certain death.

And the lull was filled with Eddie's moans. There were almost no words now, like a child in a nightmare. Then he began to call for his mother.

“He’s given up on you,” the Scot said to Charlie. It wasn’t said in an unkind way – he was just speaking the terrible truth.

His words stung Charlie and filled him with a helpless anguish. What could he do? He knew he would die for sure if he tried to help his brother again.

“Maaaaam,” Eddie cried, like an abandoned infant calling from a cot. “*Maaaaam.*”

Machine-gun fire whistled overhead and Eddie fell silent.

CHAPTER 10

Saturday 1st July, 1916
9.00 a.m.

The heat of the cloudless day did not let up and Charlie was disturbed to realise he had drunk the last of his water. His tongue was stuck to the roof of his mouth and his head throbbed with thoughts of heat and thirst. He began to doze, waking with a violent start when the fourth wave approached the German trenches.

"Why do they keep sending them over? It's sheer bloody murder," he whispered to the soldier next to him.

"Orders is orders," the lad said. "Officers have been told what to do and they're sticking to it. Bloody idiots." Then he paused for thought. "Maybe we should try to get back and warn them."

Charlie put a hand on his arm. "They can see the German lines from our trenches," he said. "They must know what's happening. Any one of us moves from here before it's dark, we're dead."

Charlie's throat felt like sandpaper. It hurt like mad to speak when he was so thirsty. He curled up into a ball and waited for the next wave of slaughter that was heading their way. He tried to suppress the helpless sob that was building inside him.

But the young soldier could not help himself. He crouched up over the rim of the crater and waved his arms in a frenzy. "Get back – you'll all ..." he yelled.

A single rifle shot cut short his words and he slumped forward.

"They're not wasting any bullets on him," the Scottish soldier said. His tone was dark. "They're saving them up for the poor sods in that fourth wave."

Charlie felt that he could bear it no longer. He curled up in a ball, just as Eddie had back in the trench all those hours ago, and placed his hands over his ears. "Make it stop," he muttered. "Dear God, make it stop."

But there was no stopping it. It went on and on. The fire from the German lines was intense, and the attack faltered just like the previous three waves.

And then something happened – something different. The British began to shell the German trenches with shrapnel. Ordinary high explosives blew up when they hit the ground. These shrapnel shells exploded in the air and scattered lethal iron pellets over soldiers on the ground.

"Whose bloody ridiculous idea was this?" the Scotsman asked. "What are they trying to do, make sure every last one of us is dead? Do they think the Germans need some help? God almighty. We've got this far and now our own artillery are going to kill us."

A shell exploded in the air above them. Charlie felt the blast suck the air from his lungs, and an instant later searing pain shot up and down his legs like jabbing white-hot wires. He heard himself scream in agony, then he fell into a deep dark tunnel.

CHAPTER 11

Sunday 2nd July, 1916
2.00 a.m.

Charlie became aware that someone was shaking him. As he came to his senses he realised he was in a very dark place. He also realised that he was in terrible pain. The sensation was like a light turning up in intensity. Dull at first and then a sudden blinding agony. He grimaced and tried not to cry out. Someone was leaning over him.

"Private, can you stand up?" a voice asked.

"I don't know," he replied. "Where am I?" His own voice was a hoarse whisper.

"Where you've been all day. Here, drink this."

Charlie felt a water bottle at his lips and gulped down as much as he could before it was taken away from him.

The water gave Charlie back some of his strength, but it didn't take away the blinding pain that pulsed behind his eyes.

"What time is it?" he asked.

"Never mind that. We've got to take you back to our lines."

"Is there still a boy on the wire?" Charlie asked. "Just in front of us?"

"Never mind that, Private," the man said. "You just worry about yourself."

Then Charlie froze in horror as he heard a German voice just to his right.

"Don't worry about him either," the man said. "Some of them are helping us."

"Hello, Tommy," a soldier in German uniform said. "You have taken one hell of a beating. But the battle is over for today."

'My God,' Charlie thought. 'I must be hallucinating.' All at once he felt powerfully dizzy and exhausted. Images and thoughts tumbled through his mind. Overwhelmed, he passed out again.

He came to with a sharp shooting pain in his legs. Someone was carrying him, dragging his broken legs through No Man's Land.

"Please can we stop?" he begged, through gritted teeth.

"I thought you might be dead, mate," the soldier carrying him said. "Of course we can stop for a minute. But then we'll have to get going. It'll be first light soon and who knows when Fritz will start firing at us again."

The man placed him gently on the ground. "You wait here," he said. "I'll go and see who else I can find."

Charlie's legs were so painful he couldn't bear to put any weight on them. He lay flat on the shattered earth and dragged himself forward with his arms, towards his own lines. All around him were dead bodies. Some didn't have a mark on them, others were torn to pieces. It was a vision straight from hell. He looked up at the night sky. For now the moon was covered by cloud, but whenever it came out, machine-gun fire burst from the German lines. He remembered the man who had spoken to him in the crater and realised that not all the Germans on the other side were prepared to be so kind.

In the dark, Charlie became aware of other men moving around – dark shadows clawing through the mud and blood in search of safety. A shot rang out from the trench in front of him and Charlie shut his eyes against the flash of the rifle. For a moment he wondered if he had turned the wrong way, but then a voice called out, "Hold your fire, we're trying to get back."

The moon glided out from behind a cloud and in its light Charlie saw the face of his friend Harry Pike, dead on the ground. His chest was a dark mess of blood, but his eyes were closed as if he were sleeping. His box Brownie camera was attached, as always, to his belt. On an impulse Charlie popped the strap button and stuffed the camera into his backpack. He knew there was a photo of Eddie in there and he wanted it to remember him by.

Charlie lay back, exhausted by the effort of crawling over to Harry and taking the camera.

When he woke up again, the sky was streaked with golden pink light. Ahead were the British trenches. He called out, but his voice was feeble and no one heard him. His terrible thirst had returned, more brutal than ever. Charlie tried to crawl forward, but his limbs had lost all their strength.

"There you are." A familiar voice – kind and practical. Charlie choked back a sob of sheer relief. "Come on, mate, almost there."

Charlie lifted his head from the ground to see the soldier who had carried him earlier.

The man picked him up again and Charlie wanted to tell him the German machine gunners would shoot them down. They must be able to see them now in the gathering dawn. He tensed, so certain he would be shot in the back that he forgot his pain. But no shots rang out and a minute later he tumbled into a filthy trench and four soldiers with red crosses on their arms carried him to the nearest first aid station. There he was laid on a stretcher and he remembered no more until he opened his eyes to see a pretty nurse leaning over him.

"He's awake now," she called to another nurse, and mopped his brow with a damp cloth.

All around seemed impossibly clean, but the first thing Charlie thought of was Eddie. He wondered with horror if his brother was still out there on the wire.

CHAPTER 12

Hastings
Sunday 2nd July, 1916

The next morning, Rose ran to the newsagent's to buy a copy of *The Times* and the *Hastings Herald*. There was nothing useful in the *Herald*, but *The Times* had the story on the front page. There had been a great attack on the Somme, the paper said, and many German prisoners had been taken. The report said in plain words and large black letters that British losses had been slight. That made Rose feel a little better. But it didn't stop her worrying.

But the following week things happened that began to unsettle her. No one got a single letter from the Front. They just stopped arriving. Many of the factory girls had husbands or sweethearts out there with the Hastings Pals and not one of them came to work with news of a letter. It must be that the Pals had been in the thick of the action.

Then one evening, as they turned up for their shift, they heard a terrible story from Mabel. Mabel's husband worked at the railway station and he said that an ambulance train had come in from France on the ferry that afternoon. When it stopped for a few moments at Hastings on its way to London someone inside had shouted out, "What station is this?"

When Mabel's husband answered "Hastings!", the injured man aboard the train said, "Hastings? The Hastings Pals ... they've been wiped out."

Then there was silence as if a nurse had come and shushed the injured man. The train had sped on its way and Mabel's husband didn't hear any more.

That story blazed round the town like wildfire. Rose went home the next morning after her night shift, and she wrote Charlie the longest letter she had ever written. She told him how much she thought of him, and how much she loved him. She told him she wanted him to come back to her, more than anything else in the world. She folded the sheets of thin paper into their envelope, then walked to the post box, her heart heavy with dread that he was already dead.

As the weeks went by, a slow trickle of letters from wounded soldiers began to arrive. They didn't say anything useful. They were those awful printed postcards where soldiers weren't allowed to write anything apart from their name – they just crossed out the words that didn't apply to them.

I have/have not been wounded.

most of them said.

At the bottom of the cards it said

If you write anything else on this communication it will be destroyed.

Rose prayed every night that she would at least get a card like that, rather than one to tell her that Charlie was dead. But in between her prayers, she worried that Charlie had lost an arm or a leg, or his sight, or had been horribly scarred. She had seen soldiers in the street with damaged faces. Some even walked around with a tin mask over their faces to spare passers-by the horror of their mangled features. If Charlie came home like one of those poor men, did she love him enough to look after him for the rest of his life? And what if he had damaged his hands, or had them blown away? She'd always loved the way he played the piano, and sometimes he even sang to her as his hands moved over the keys. In his letters he had often told her that he planned to make his fortune writing songs for the music halls, when this war was over.

Then, over the next few weeks, the telegrams with the black borders began to arrive. Every day at the factory one of the girls would be missing, and they'd all know why.

At long last, Rose heard some news. Charlie's mother, a sweet little woman she only knew as Mrs Taylor, banged on her door. The banging roused Rose from a deep sleep after a night shift. She ran downstairs and opened the door with trembling hands. Mrs Taylor held an envelope out to her. It didn't have a black border. It was one of those postcards and it only said –

I have/~~have not~~ been wounded.

Rose let Mrs Taylor hug her, neither woman saying a word. As she left Mrs Taylor said, "He'll be back here soon enough. He'll be so pleased to see you again." Rose returned to bed and cried herself to sleep. Whether it was from relief or worry she never really knew.

A week later, Charlie arrived home on one of those ambulance trains and spent a month in the local hospital. By then, the *Hastings Herald* was full of column after column of photos of the boys who had been killed on the Somme.

Rose went to see him as soon as she was allowed. His face lit up when he saw her, but she couldn't hug him – his wounds were too painful. But at least his handsome face was all right. Apart from his eyes. They hadn't been damaged or anything. But they darted around, never settling on anything. They used to twinkle, she remembered. As if he was always smiling at the world. Not any more. And when she stared into those eyes, like she used to do when they were out courting, it was like he was a thousand miles away.

One afternoon when she visited, she took him the picture of Eddie that had been printed in the *Herald* that day.

"Look, Charlie," she said. "It says he's 'missing in action', not dead. We can still have some hope that he's alive, can't we?"

But Charlie said nothing. He just shook his head and turned away from her to face the wall.

A month later they sent Charlie back to France.

Every morning Rose got home from work expecting to hear that Mrs Taylor had received the telegram with the black border.

CHAPTER 13

Friday 1st July, 2016

The boys wander back from the beach with Grandma Rose and they sit round the kitchen table with a jug of iced water, recovering from the heat of the day. Eddie has caught a little too much sun and his mum has made him rub sunburn cream into his face and arms.

"Show Mum the photo we found, Grandma," Charlie says.

Grandma Rose takes the photo out of its cardboard folder and looks at it. "There's my dad," she says. "And there's his brother, Eddie. My mum – that's your great-grandma Rose –

told me they patched him up and he fought for another two months in that battle. He never told her any more than that, and she was his wife for forty years. He was gassed in early November and they had the decency to send him home after that. My mum was convinced that being gassed saved his life, but even so he never could climb the stairs without completely wearing himself out. I'm surprised he lived till his sixties."

Grandma Rose pauses, and they all wait while she gathers her thoughts.

"When he came back he married my mum and they bought this house," she says. "Then my sister came to live here with them when they grew old. That's your Aunty Lily. She stayed after they passed away. Just think, if he'd been killed on the Somme like so many of his pals, I would never have been born and you would never have been born, and none of us would be sitting here now ..."

"Think about that too much and you'd start to go a bit mad," Charlie says.

Grandma Rose stares at something none of them can see. "He was a funny man, my dad," she says. "My mum had a hard life with him. He was a difficult man to like. Very closed up. She said he'd changed so much when he came back, he'd lost his spark. But that's what they said about all the boys who came back from the trenches. I don't think he ever forgave himself for coming back on his own, without his brother Eddie."

Grandma Rose gets up from the table and goes over to sit on the stool at the piano. She smooths her hands over its oak lid.

"He spent most evenings sitting here, at this piano," she says with a sigh. "Sometimes he even came down in the middle of the night, to play these sad little melodies. He must have found some comfort in it. Other times, he'd vanish at night. I'd hear the door go and think he must have a fancy woman, but he'd tell Mother he'd had another of his nightmares and just went to walk the streets until he felt tired enough to sleep again. I thought that was a pretty feeble excuse, but then my mum told me a lot of the wives said their husbands did that. You'd peep out of the window at four in the morning almost any day, and there'd be someone tramping around." She gazes out of the kitchen window, remembering.

"Poor old Dad," Grandma Rose says. "You always felt he had a terrible secret he could never share ..."

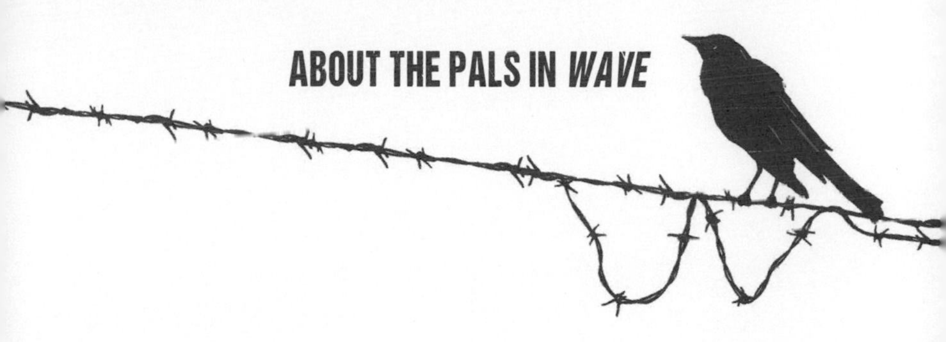

ABOUT THE PALS IN *WAVE*

The two brothers in *Wave* – Charlie and Eddie Taylor – are soldiers in the First World War, and they fight with the "Hastings Pals" battalion. I made up this particular battalion for my story – it never existed, but dozens of other Pals battalions did.

The idea of the Pals battalions was simple. In what was then known as the Great War, men could volunteer for the army with their friends and all serve together in the same unit. And so Pals Battalions were formed, of men who were all from the same school, factory or town. The idea was hugely popular at the start of the war, when young men thought going off to fight the Germans in France and Belgium would be a great adventure they could experience with their friends and neighbours. Instead, they faced the mud, squalor and horror of the trenches.

The Pals idea turned out to be a disaster. In the mill town of Accrington in the north-west of England, for example, 800 young men joined the "Accrington Pals". On the opening day of the Battle of the Somme, which is where the action in this story takes place, over 600 of them were killed before the morning was out. The town was devastated. At times of heavy fighting, this was a story repeated all over the country, and across Commonwealth countries like Canada, South Africa, New Zealand and Australia. The British Army now distributes men from the same region throughout its various regiments.

Paul Dowswell

Our books are tested
for children and young people by
children and young people.

Thanks to everyone who consulted on
a manuscript for their time and effort in
helping us to make our books better
for our readers.

An "emotional, vivid and superbly related" novel of World War One and the Gallipoli Campaign, inspired by a true story.

"I promised I'd take care of him and that we'd always be together," I gabbled. "He's too small to cope on his own."

When Bert and Frank Barker are taken from the Children's Home in London, the priests promise them a better life in Australia. But what really awaits is hard work, separation, and the realisation that no one cares if they live or die.

Then war breaks out, and fate brings the brothers together again – in a place more horrific than either of them could ever imagine.